Gal and Noa's Daddies

Shosh Pinkas

Illustrated by Julia Filipone–Erez

Gal and Noa's Daddies

Shosh Pinkas

Illustrated by Julia Filipone-Erez
Translation: Michal Emanuel & Rachel Madar
Editing: Suzanne Klein

Production: www.notssa.com

To Gal and Noa,
my beloved granddaughters

Gal and Noa, my granddaughters, were born in Mumbai, India, on August 30, 2010, through the process of surrogacy.

The joy and excitement I felt at their birth was tinged with concerns for the future. As time went by, I became more and more preoccupied by the thought of what their daddies would tell them when they were old enough to ask how they came into this world.

I asked myself: What would I tell them? And no less important, how would the nursery school teachers, the other children, or their parents react when they understood that Gal and Noa had two fathers but no mother.

I wanted to avoid embarrassing situations or attempts to avoid the topic.

As I couldn't find an acceptable answer in any of the existing children's books, I decided to write a book myself: a book that would give an authentic description of the experience of my son, Itai, and his partner, Yoav, from the moment they decided to have children through surrogacy.

This book is dedicated to dear Itai and Yoav, who make their way in the world with their heads held high, and who are raising Gal and Noa with so much love and skill.

Grandma Shosh

"Let's play Daddies," called Gal from the swing.
"Don't be silly," laughed Mary. "There's no such thing!"
"Of course there is!" Noa jumped up right away.
"It's just like our family. So come on, let's play!"

"You made that up!" said Nill, getting mad.
"There isn't a family with more than one dad.
Boys don't marry boys; don't be absurd.
That's the silliest thing that I've ever heard!"

Lisa piped up, all of a sudden,
"That's just like in the house of my cousin!
They have a dog and a cat, a goldfish and bunnies,
Identical twin girls and also two mommies."

They started to play but it wasn't quite clear,
Not to Nill, or to Mary, or even to Amir.
"Who does what in a family like yours?"
"How do you decide who does which chores?"
"Who cuts the salad, cooks meals, and bakes cakes?"
"Who buys groceries and fixes stuff that breaks?"

Noa shouted, "Quiet everyone! Let me explain.
Then we can all start playing again."
Gal cut her off and said she wanted to tell
How their family works, which it does, very well.
But the kids were all shouting. They needed to see,
"What do you call them: Daddy A and Daddy B?!"

Gal and Noa laughed and cried out, "No, no!
One daddy is Yoav, so he's Daddy-Yo.
Our other daddy's name is Itai,
So of course he's Daddy-I."

When the girls came home to their daddies that day,
They were very excited and had so much to say
About the game and the questions and also the fight.
They wanted their daddies to put it all right.
Gal said that actually, she didn't really know
How she and Noa were born a few years ago.

The daddies hugged them and said, "First we eat.
Daddy-Yo's cooked up a very nice treat.
Once Daddy-I clears up, and the kitchen is clean,
We'll sit on the sofa and explain the whole thing."
And so, after supper, they cuddled up with the cats,
And talked about all kinds of this's and that's.

They sat together quietly for a minute or two,
Cuddling, snuggling, and planning things to do.
Then the two daddies told how it began,
Before they became such a cute little clan.

This is the story of Daddy–I and Daddy–Yo,
Who fell in love with each other a long time ago.
They loved each other a lot and lived happily together
So they wanted to marry and stay like that forever.

Now boys marrying boys was something quite new
So marrying each other wasn't easy to do.
But they didn't give up; they knew how to proceed.
To marry in Canada, they flew at full speed.

They came back home to live happily ever after
And soon decided it was time for children's laughter.
They knew it would be a long life decision,
But they had enough love to take on such a mission.

To make a baby, there are a few things you need:
A woman's teeny egg and a man's tiny seed.
When the egg meets the seed, a baby begins
And that's one of life's most beautiful things.

The baby begins life as a tiny embryo
But it needs a mommy's tummy in order to grow
So if two daddies want to have babies one day
They'll need a little help, but they can find a way.

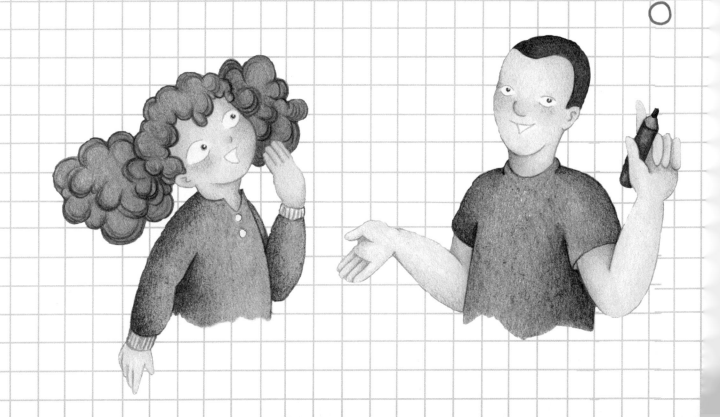

The daddies found people, kind and good
Who helped them in every way that they could.
With the help of some doctors, loving and smart,
They got eggs from a lady with a very kind heart.
Another doctor helped each egg meet a seed,
So now the embryos had nearly all they would need.

Far away in India lived another nice lady,
And she had agreed to carry their babies.
The embryos were gently placed in her womb,
Where they would grow until they ran out of room.

The daddies flew to India to meet the nice lady
And thank her for helping them have babies.
They made sure she felt good and had lots of rest,
Ate up her vegetables and had everything that was best.

When the lady's tummy was round and the babies were due,
Grandma Shosh hopped on a plane and away to India she flew.
But what a surprise! Just as her plane landed,
She was thrilled to hear her family had expanded.

The uncles and aunts were thrilled and cried "Oooooh!"
As not one little baby had been born, but twooo!
The girls on the couch got very excited.
This was their story; they were truly delighted!

Sitting in the living room, the girls nodded their heads.
With a smile on their lips, they were ready for bed.
The daddies picked up both girls with a gentle touch,
Letting them know that they loved them so much.

The girls gave tired kisses amid sleepy sighs
And finally shut their beautiful eyes.
Still they managed to whisper, "Good night and sleep tight.
For us this family is exactly right!"

Made in the USA
Las Vegas, NV
03 February 2023

66774412R00017